D1442208

Dedicated to those who strive to protect Hawaii's ocean environment and unique wildlife.

The Goodnight Gecko
Gecko Hide and Seek
The Whale Who Wanted to be Small
The Brave Little Turtle
Tikki Turtle's Quest
The Shark Who Learned a Lesson
The Wonderful Journey
A Whale's Tale
The Gift of Aloha
How the Geckos Learned to Chirp
Happy as a Dolphin
The Rainbow Mermaids of Hawaii

For more information and fun activities, visit Gill's website:
www.HawaiianChildrensBooks.com

 Find Us on **FaceBook**: Gill McBarnet - HawaiianChildrensBooks.com

First published 2016 by Ruwanga Trading
ISBN 978-0-9701528-5-5
Printed in China by Everbest Printing Co., Ltd

BOOK ENQUIRIES AND ORDERS:
Booklines Hawaii, a division of The Islander Group
269 Pali'i Street
Mililani, Hawaii 96789
Phone: 808-676-0116, ext.206
Fax: 808-676-5156
Toll Free: 1-877-828-4852
Website: www.islandergroup.com

Hoku
the Seal's Three Wishes

Written and illustrated by Gill McBarnet

Hoku was a little Monk seal who lived with his mother on the warm beaches and in the blue ocean that surrounds Hawaii.

Hoku had everything a little seal needs. A shallow reef

with colorful corals, and whenever he was sleepy...

...he could pull himself up onto a golden beach and sleep next to his mother, and drink milk from his mama to help him grow big and strong.

In his dreams, Hoku always wished for things that most little seals don't wish for. In one dream he wished he could fly! "You should be happy with who you are and what you have," his mother told him. But Hoku always wanted MORE!

One sunny day when he was dreaming, his mother said "Hoku, I'm going to cool off in the ocean. Wait here for me, and I'll be right back."

But being a curious little seal, Hoku wanted to see what was further down the beach, so he didn't wait for his mama. He wanted to explore!

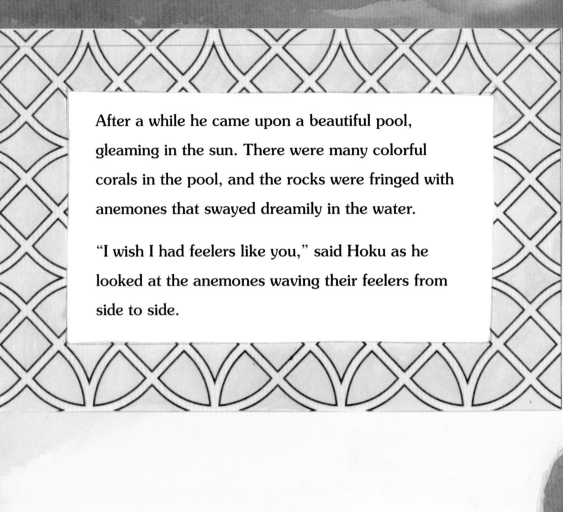

After a while he came upon a beautiful pool, gleaming in the sun. There were many colorful corals in the pool, and the rocks were fringed with anemones that swayed dreamily in the water.

"I wish I had feelers like you," said Hoku as he looked at the anemones waving their feelers from side to side.

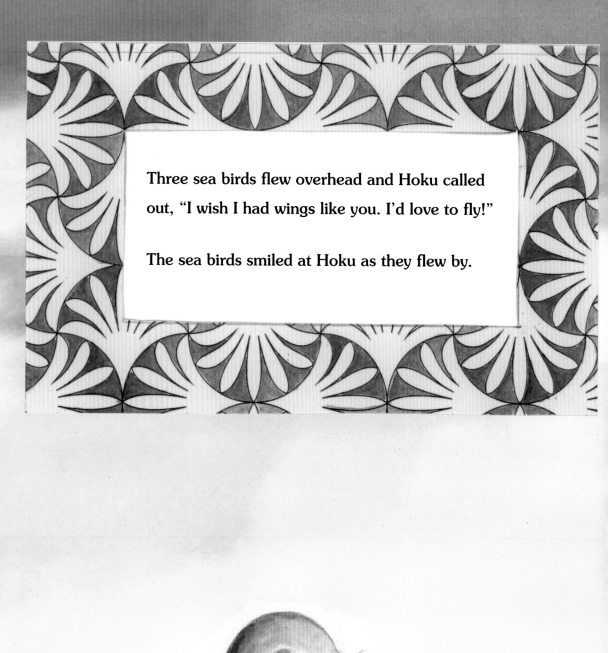

Three sea birds flew overhead and Hoku called out, "I wish I had wings like you. I'd love to fly!"

The sea birds smiled at Hoku as they flew by.

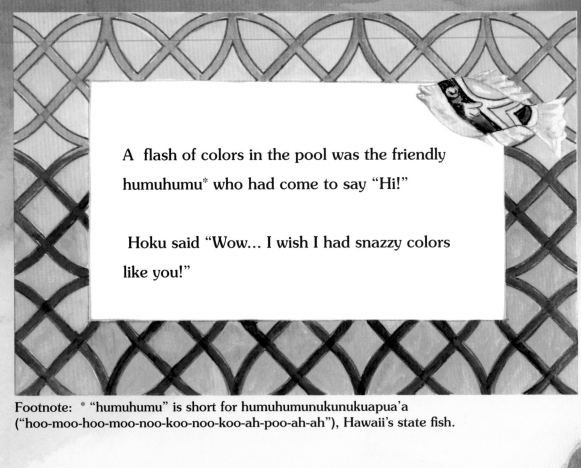

A flash of colors in the pool was the friendly humuhumu* who had come to say "Hi!"

Hoku said "Wow... I wish I had snazzy colors like you!"

Footnote: * "humuhumu" is short for humuhumunukunukuapua'a ("hoo-moo-hoo-moo-noo-koo-noo-koo-ah-poo-ah-ah"), Hawaii's state fish.

Hoku felt a tingling and rumbling in his body and all of a sudden ... "PUFF!" There was a flash of light and Hoku felt very strange.

Hoku looked at his reflection in the pool but he was no longer a plain little seal. He now had feelers on his head, wings instead of flippers, and a colorful body. "Oh my!" cried Hoku "What happened?"

The old goat fish said "This is no ordinary pool, Hoku. It is a WISHING POOL, where wishes come true. You must wish wisely, because you are only allowed three wishes".

Hoku flapped his wings, trying to fly - but he wasn't able to get off the beach because he was rather a HEAVY little seal.

"Sorry Hoku," called the sea birds "...we wish you could join us, but you need to be feather-light all over if you want to fly."

Hoku looked at the anemones in the wishing pool. "I can wave my feelers like the anemones," he said. But the more his feelers bobbled about, the more dizzy he started to feel and soon he was wobbling from side to side.

Two little clown fish started giggling, and one of the clown fish said "Sorry we can't stop giggling Hoku, but your feelers look so funny!"

Hoku wasn't having fun like the fish, the anemones – or the sea birds. Being dizzy with wings that won't fly and feelers that bobble about was not as exciting as he had thought it would be.

Hoku looked down at his body, and he realized how much he missed his soft brown fur that kept him nice and warm. With a sob, he said "I don't want to have wings or feelers or bright colors anymore. I just wish I was ME again!"

But nothing happened. The old goat fish said "Once you have used up your three wishes, you're not allowed anymore wishes."

"Oh no! What am I going to do when mama gets back?"
"Hide yourself in seaweed..." said the goat fish, doing his best to help.

When mother seal returned, Hoku had covered himself in seaweed and was peeping at his mama from under all the seaweed. Mama said with a chuckle: "Come on Hoku. Shake off the seaweed and come and snooze with me again!" Mama rolled over to snooze, and Hoku said "What can I do ? Mama will be angry when she wakes up and sees I'm not a seal anymore."

The goat fish said "Roll in the sand, so you are covered in sand and shells." Hoku rolled and rolled, but he wasn't able to hide his feelers, wings and colors. "Oh dear" said Hoku "… mama's waking up from her nap. What can I do NOW?"

"Wash off in the pool and tell your mama the truth," said the old goat fish.

So Hoku washed off the sand, shells and seaweed, and mama's flippers flew up in surprise as she exclaimed "Hoku! What happened to you, my precious little seal?"

"I'm sorry mama" said Hoku, "I was wishing for feelers like the anemones, wings like the seabirds, and a colorful body like humuhumu…"

"Oh Hoku, you know I always tell you how perfect you are as my little seal…"

"But look! Here's Olu the wise old turtle. Perhaps he can tell us what to do." Sure enough, up swam Olu the oldest and wisest of turtles, and Olu listened to Hoku's story.

"Hmm" said Olu. "It is true you have used up your three wishes, Hoku, but if your mama hasn't made any wishes by the wishing pool, perhaps SHE would like to make a wish…"

So mama seal wished for her little seal to be just the way he was, before wishing for feelers, wings – and a brightly colored body. In a rumble and a "PUFF", Hoku was back to being a little seal again.

That night, as they snuggled under a starry sky, mama said: "Hoku O Ke Kai, my little Star of the Sea, I love you just the way you are," and from that day onwards Hoku was happy to be a seal with soft fur, fast flippers and big shiny eyes that twinkled like stars.